DANNY ORLIS
AND THE
ROCK POINT REBEL

DANNY ORLIS

AND THE

ROCK POINT REBEL

BERNARD PALMER

Please note that several books in the Danny Orlis series are published by Sword of the Lord Publications and are available for purchase on their website, www.swordbooks.com.

Aneko Press *Youth*

www.anekopress.com

Aneko Press, Life Sentence Publishing, and our logos are trademarks of
Life Sentence Publishing, Inc.
203 E. Birch Street
P.O. Box 652
Abbotsford, WI 54405
JUVENILE FICTION / Religious / Christian / Action & Adventure
Paperback ISBN: 979-8-88936-090-2
eBook ISBN: 979-8-88936-091-9
10 9 8 7 6 5 4 3 2 1
Available where books are sold

CONTENTS

CHAPTER 1

A MEETING IN THE CAFÉ

Bill Anderson left the schoolhouse alone, and, leaning into the bitter February wind, he made his way to the parking lot and his car. While he drove home, he thought about the evening ahead.

Neither of his parents would be home. It was payday, and his dad would stop off at the nearest bar and try to slosh down his troubles with beer. And it was bingo day at the club, so his mother wouldn't be home until midnight, which was just as well; at least she wouldn't be yelling to him and Val about their dad and what a worthless, drunken bum he was.

He parked in the driveway in front of the garage, gathered his books from the seat beside him, and got out. When Bill stood, he was half a head taller than his dad. A robust, muscular six-foot-two, Bill had been a steamroller for the Northwest High School offensive football unit the fall before. His square-cut features were familiar to those who watched the local sports news. Some predicted he would be tagged by one of the major universities, and others were going so far as to say he would make the pro circuit when he finished his college career.

However, such talk didn't interest Bill much anymore. There were other things he was concerned about now that he knew what it was like to walk with Jesus Christ. He had been trying to share his faith with his parents, searching for words to explain what Jesus meant to him and how He had changed his life. They only listened with bewilderment, unable to understand Bill.

They liked the fact that Bill wasn't hanging around with the same old crowd and hadn't been to a beer bash for months, but they didn't know how it happened; nor were they sure they liked the things that went with the change.

"We want you to live your own life, Bill," his mother said. "And we're glad you're not running with a rough crowd. But do you have to be so – well, fanatical about it?"

At first he protested that he wasn't a fanatic and tried to make her understand that it was great to have Jesus Christ in control of his life. He soon saw that was useless, however. She had already made up her mind he was making a fool of himself by being so "religious." The more he said, the more convinced she became that she was right.

His dad had much the same idea, although he didn't say much about it. The truth was, his dad didn't get a chance to say a great deal about anything around the house unless liquor loosened his tongue. When that happened, his self-restraint disappeared, and he was strident and short-tempered. Drunk, he was no longer afraid of his wife's sharp, unpredictable tongue and was apt to throw the furniture around or give somebody a black eye if he was crossed.

Bill and his fourteen-year-old sister, Valerie, had long since learned to anticipate those occasions. Experience taught them to be wary on payday or their mom's day for bingo. When the two happened at the same time, they knew what the end result would be. Their dad would come home drunk, if he came home at all, and their mother would be defensive and belligerent. There was always a good fight. The kids found it best to stay out of the way.

Mentally, Bill checked the money in his wallet. He had to buy another five gallons of gas and pay for a tire repair, but he had enough extra to take Val out for pizza. Later he could take her to a game or the library or just for a ride – anything to stay out of the house until bedtime. He could have gone out alone, but he didn't like the idea of leaving Val to face their dad when he came staggering in.

When Bill entered the house, Val was curled up in a threadbare chair in the living room, watching a music video and trying to study. The volume was turned up until the beat rattled the windows.

"Hi."

She looked up.

"Want to go out with me and get a pizza?" he asked, flopping on the couch across from her.

"Where's Mom?" she asked.

"This is her bingo day. Remember?"

"Oh, so that explains why the sink's full of dirty dishes." She wrinkled her nose in disgust. "And the garbage hasn't been taken out."

"I'll take it out. Then we'll go to Gina's. How's that?"

As they got into the car, Bill saw their dad driving up to the house. "We'd better get a move on if we don't want him to catch us."

She noted the erratic approach of the car.

"Drunk again!" Her voice rose angrily. "I don't care if I never see this crummy place again!"

Bill saw the hurt come over her face, and his heart ached for her. There were times when he felt just like Val. If it weren't that he was a Christian and had a sister who needed looking after, he'd split and nobody in Rock Point would ever see him again. He wouldn't stick around another minute and take what he had to take from his parents.

Bill had a make-up test to do the next morning and had to be at school right at eight o'clock. Ordinarily Val rode with Bill, but she fooled around so long he had to leave for school before she was ready. He tried to explain to her, but she didn't give him the opportunity. Her anger flashed.

"I suppose you've got to get to school early so you can pray!" she retorted.

He left without replying to her.

After he was gone, she stood before the mirror, her temper surging. *If he thought I was interested in that religion of his, he'd sure have hung around. He'd have stayed there all day.* Just because she wasn't stupid enough to buy any of it, he didn't care whether she got to school on time or not.

Bill ran off just to be mean, she decided. If he really meant all that junk about being a different person, he'd have waited a few minutes for her. He talked a lot, but he had already shown her there was nothing to that church business. *Just wait until he tries to push it on me again!* She'd let him know what she thought about it.

She ran the comb through her hair again and bounced into the kitchen to get a bowl of cereal. Her mother was upset. She was nervous and her voice had a sharp edge.

"Val," she whined, "do you know what time it is?"

There was no answer.

"You'd better hurry or you'll be late." Mrs. Anderson appeared in the doorway, her frail figure hidden within her dirty robe.

"You can take me, can't you, Mom?"

"I told you yesterday that I've taken you to school for the last time. You should have ridden with Bill."

"I was going to, but he ran off and left me."

"Don't come to me complaining. I've got troubles enough of my own with that father of yours. I can't be bothered with getting you to school on time. If you can't get around in time to ride with your brother, you'll have to walk."

Val hadn't wanted to argue with her mother that morning, but her voice raised and before she realized it, they were fighting bitterly. It did not end until Mrs. Anderson stormed into her bedroom and slammed the door. Listening from the hall, Val could hear sobbing.

On other occasions the sound of her mother's crying tore her apart and she would go in to apologize contritely. But this time it was different. The argument hadn't been her fault, she reasoned.

She'd only asked her mother to give her a ride to school. There was nothing wrong with that. Most of the kids in her grade got rides to school with somebody.

She didn't know why her mother had to keep yelling at her all the time. Why couldn't she be like the mothers of other kids? All she thought about was bingo and those silly friends of hers. She didn't have time to cook or wash the dishes or keep the house clean.

Struggling into her coat, Val stormed out of the

house and across the street in the direction of the school.

The trouble with her parents was that they didn't think anything of her. They didn't love her, let alone care whether she got to school on time or not. Her mother was a bingo addict. She kidded about starting a "Bingo Anonymous," but it really wasn't a joke anymore. Now Bill had become a religious fanatic and spent most of his time trying to convert her.

Impulsively she turned away from the school, heading toward town. *Why go to school? Nobody cares whether I get there or not. What I really want to do is get my clothes and go so far away they'll never be able to find me.* A tear burned a path down her cheek.

She didn't suppose they would even notice she was gone. She knew her mom wouldn't if there happened to be enough bingo games to keep her busy. Her dad wouldn't, either, as long as he had money enough for another glass of beer.

The more she thought about leaving, the more appealing the idea became. She didn't have any particular destination in mind. *I'll just take off – anywhere – just as long as I can get out of this crummy house and this stupid town. I'll go so far away I won't be able to find anyone who has even heard of Rock Point.*

Val was so disturbed as she walked that she didn't think about the time or even where she was going. She must have walked twenty or thirty minutes when, impulsively, she slipped inside a greasy, little side-street café with half a dozen stools at the counter and a row of tables strung along the length of the narrow building.

Just inside the door she paused and looked around. There were no other customers in the place at the moment – just one waitress and the cook. But that suited her fine. She wanted to be alone to think things out. On another impulse, she stepped back out to a shop on the street. She bought a package of cigarettes and then strolled back inside to a table. She had only smoked a few times and didn't particularly like the bitter taste of cigarettes, but in buying them, she suddenly felt free and grownup.

Val ordered a coke and watched the ice cubes melt. No one said anything to her when she lit her cigarette, so she finished one and was lighting another when the door opened and a gangling, long-legged guy slouched in. His hair was long and uncombed. His jeans were dirty, and his youthful face was hidden beneath a beard. He appeared older than Val.

He stood just inside the steamed door, his legs apart slightly and a faint smile on his mouth, as though he didn't care about anything. *His parents probably don't shove him around, that's easy to see. He's not the kind who takes being bossed by anybody. He's really cool.* Val watched him admiringly. She wished he would come over and talk to her. She could go for a guy like him. That was exactly the kind of person she was going to become.

She remembered a flag they had studied in history. It showed a coiled rattlesnake and carried the words, "Don't Tread on Me!" That was going to be her motto from now on. She'd be her own boss and anyone who tried to run her life would have to be prepared. She wasn't taking it anymore!

He turned to leave and then caught sight of her. His face lit up, and a grin appeared. She smiled and waved her cigarette at him in what she hoped was a sophisticated gesture inviting him to join her. He sauntered carelessly back to the table where Val was sitting.

"Hi." She spoke to him, keeping the faintest hint of a smile in place.

"You look lonely and all uptight," he said.

"How did you guess?"

He started to sit down across from her but stopped, resting both hands on the table. "It's okay if I sit down, isn't it?"

"Could I stop you?"

"I guess not." He picked up the package and took a cigarette from it. "Thanks."

"Help yourself. There are more where that one came from."

He said nothing more until he lit his cigarette and pulled the smoke into his lungs.

"There's not as much kick to this as some other stuff I've been smoking, but I guess it's the best you've got."

Val shivered. She had met some kids at school who tried weed, but he was different. *This guy has been around. He probably smokes hash, too. He looks like the kind of guy who'd do anything.* She was afraid but also excited.

"What's a cute kid like you doing all alone in a dump like this?"

She laughed without humor. "If you want the truth, I'm trying to decide why I didn't go to school this morning."

"And what you'll tell teacher when you go back this afternoon. Is that right?"

"Now you're making fun of me."

"I just know what you're thinking, that's all."

"How could somebody like you know?"

He reached over and laid his hands on hers. "Paul Keller knows because he faced up to that one a long time ago. And let me fill you in. It's a bad trip to get hung up on."

His remark struck a responsive chord.

"And what did you do?"

"To tell you the truth, I split. I wasn't having a teacher tell me what to do! I'd had my fill of that at home!"

CHAPTER 2

VAL SPEAKS HER MIND

Val almost panicked as she realized his show of understanding was drawing tears to her eyes. She mustn't cry in front of this cool guy. Quickly she crushed her cigarette. Hearing the frustration and rebellion voiced by Paul ignited the anger that lay within her.

"I have the same problem!" she exploded. "Nobody at home cares anything about me. I'm just like part of the furniture until they decide they've got to have somebody to kick around!"

He smiled loftily at her.

"I know exactly what's bugging you. I went through the same bad scene myself as long as I was stupid enough to stay at home and let them wipe their feet on me." Paul's grin came back, and he patted her hand reassuringly. "But I finally wised up and split.

You could do the same thing if you really are fed up with it."

She lit another cigarette.

"It's easy for you to talk that way," she countered, anxious to make him understand how tough things were for her at home. "Dad's smashed half the time, and when Mom isn't playing bingo, she's bawling about Dad or giving me a bad time."

"I know it's a hassle," Paul told her. "I've been through everything you've been through and more too. The last time I was home my old man stormed so loud everyone in town could hear him. 'Get your hair cut! Clean up! Get rid of those grubby clothes so you can get a job. Quit smokin' weed or I'll turn you over to the cops!' I got the whole load. Finally, I packed my stuff. I don't take anything off anybody!"

Val had never expected to find anyone who was so understanding. Paul was the first person she'd ever met who could see why she didn't want to go to school. Everybody else, except the kids she ran around with, tried to give her that guff about doing what her parents and the teachers said. But compared to Paul, even her best friends were disgusting. They weren't really honest. They complained enough about the way they got treated by their parents, but that was the end of it. They didn't do anything except talk.

Paul talked, too, but he also did something. When his parents started putting too much pressure on him, he dropped out of school and took off. They soon found out they couldn't push him around.

Admiration gleamed in her eyes as she looked across the table at him. *I wonder if his name really is Paul Keller?* She suspected it might not be, but that didn't make any difference to her. Names are only status symbols, he told her.

They sat in the cafe for a long time talking. The waitress and the cook began to watch them. Val wouldn't have noticed until it was too late, but Paul knew it wouldn't be too long until they were asked to leave.

Paul leaned forward. "We'd better split," he said, keeping his voice down. "If we don't, they'll call the cops and we'll be hauled down to the station and have to answer a pile of stupid questions."

Fear appeared on her face. "Do you really think so?"

"If we stick around here, I *know* it's going to happen. And I don't care to have them get onto me right now."

Val felt real panic. Maybe she didn't want to go to school or be ordered around by her parents, but she didn't want to get into big trouble either. "You haven't broken the law, have you?"

He laughed. "That wouldn't make any difference to you, would it?"

Val hesitated. She didn't dare let Paul know how she felt. *He'd probably leave if he knew I'm scared about breaking the law.* Suddenly what he thought about her meant more than anything else.

"No," she lied, "it wouldn't make any difference. I don't want to see you get busted, that's all."

"They're not going to bust me unless they catch me doing drugs," he replied. "And I'm careful that nobody except my friends find out about that."

Val glowed inwardly. She had just met Paul and already he considered her close enough as a friend to share such privileged information. But knowing he used drugs also gave her an uneasiness.

He stood abruptly.

"I'll see you outside after you pay your tab. Meet me in the parking lot, and I'll give you a lift."

Although he said he would take her where she wanted to go, he didn't mention it again when they got in the car. Instead, they rode around the rest of the morning just talking about her problems. Val hadn't realized how much it would help her to have someone who would listen.

At noon they went to a little truck stop on the far side of Rock Point where no one would recognize her, and they had hamburgers. Paul didn't have money enough to pay for them, but Val had a few dollars in her pocket. *I can't expect him to pay for my hamburger and coke when he is so anxious to listen to my troubles.* She didn't even mind paying for his.

Reluctantly Val looked at her watch. It was time for her to go back to school for her afternoon classes.

She didn't want to leave Paul. She had enjoyed herself with him that morning. *But skipping morning classes is bad enough. Dad and Mom would half kill me if I stayed out all day.*

"Sorry," she told him, "but I've got to run."

Scorn filled his eyes. "And just what do you figure on doing this afternoon?"

"I've got to get to school."

"Did I hear you right?" he demanded. "Did you say you're going to school this afternoon after all the things you've been complaining to me about? Didn't all my expert advice mean anything to you?"

Val laughed defensively. "I'll get skinned as it is."

"That's the trouble with your kind. You get uptight, but you still let them hassle you! What am I going to have to say to you to get you to stand up for your rights?"

"I–I've never skipped school before," she admitted nervously.

"That's all the more reason why you ought to do a good job of it while you're at it. You don't know parents like I do. They're all alike. They'll run over you as long as you let 'em. You've got to stand up to them. Don't let them hammer you into their neat, little mold. Show them you're an individual and have a mind of your own! If you don't, they'll plan your whole future for you. You'll never be able to get on your own!"

He hadn't talked very long before he convinced Val

that she should spend the rest of the afternoon with him. Convincing her wasn't very hard to do because that was what she really preferred. All the gloom of the morning had disappeared. She had never been with such an exciting person. Before she was aware of it, the afternoon was almost over, and it was time for school to be out. He glanced at his watch.

"Time's up," he announced firmly. "I've got to get you home so I can split."

The way he talked, the day was ended and they would never meet again. The thought panicked her.

"Where are you going?"

He shrugged indifferently.

"I don't know."

"You've got some idea," she persisted.

"I haven't decided yet." He glanced quickly at her. "That's one thing you're going to find out about me before we've known each other very long. I never make up my mind about anything until I decide to do it. I'm free, kid. I'm free!"

She was both disturbed and drawn by his independence. She wanted desperately to know where he was going and when she would see him again. He didn't just talk about getting out from under his parents' control, he did it. She knew she would never be happy until she did the same.

She was almost afraid to suggest that he let her out a block from her home. She couldn't let him know she still cared what her parents would think. But he suggested it himself.

"I don't want to get you into any more trouble at home than you've got already, Val." His voice was almost tender. "You're too sweet a kid to have someone on your neck all the time."

He swung over to the curb, and she got out gratefully. *He doesn't see me as a little kid. He respects me as a person. And maybe he likes me just a little bit.* They had to separate, she knew, but she was reluctant.

"Will–will I see you again?" she asked, almost afraid to put the question into words, as though the forming of them might be enough to drive him away.

He winked at her.

"You know it, babe!"

He pulled the door shut behind her and jammed the accelerator to the floor. She watched as his car screeched around the corner and roared away, still gathering speed. After he had disappeared, she still stared up the empty street.

It had been a great day.

If Paul was around all the time, putting up with Mom and Dad wouldn't be half so bad. But in spite of what he had said, Val wasn't sure whether she would ever see him again. She was left to face conditions at home without him. All her troubles rushed back.

Several houses away, Val stopped walking and almost turned in the other direction. Her mother was probably waiting in a fury for her to come home so she could pounce on her about not being in school that day. She would already know, of course. The principal's office always phoned home to see if the absentees were ill.

Well, Val decided, *if I'm going to catch it, I might as well go ahead and get it over with.*

She pulled herself up tall and strode up on the porch and into the house.

"Mom!" she called. "Mom!"

There was no answer.

She went on into the kitchen. She didn't know whether to be relieved or worried. Her mother ought to be home. This was one of the days of the week she was always there.

"Mom!" Impatience lifted her voice half an octave.

Only then did she see the note on the kitchen table.

"Mable and I are going to Denver for a special bingo party. We should be back by the time school's out. In case we're not, I've left food for you in the fridge. Be a darling, Val, and warm it up for Dad and Bill. Love, Mom."

Val read the note a second time, miserably. *She didn't say anything about me getting anything to eat. All she cares about is Bill and Dad! As far as she's concerned, I'm not even a daughter. I'm just an unpaid servant.*

And she thought her mother would care if she quit school! That wouldn't make any difference to her! *Nothing I do makes any difference as long as I'm around to get food out of the refrigerator and warm it up for Bill and Dad so she can play an extra game of bingo.*

Tears flooded Val's eyes. She went into her room and threw herself across her bed. She forgot that she had been spared an angry confrontation. Instead, a feeling of being unwanted swept over her. *Paul was right! The sooner I get my things together and split, the better it will be for everybody.*

CHAPTER 3

PAUL COMES BACK

That night Val could think of little else than Paul Keller. He was the coolest guy she had ever been around. A little on the wild side, maybe, but that only made him more exciting.

I'll probably never see him again. He wouldn't want to have anything to do with me when he can go out with older, more sophisticated women. But I have to see him again if I can. I have to let him know how much he means to me.

The next night when school was out, she went over to the little side street café where she had met Paul and sat in the same booth for over an hour. The waitress asked Val where he was.

"Your boyfriend coming around today?" she wanted to know. The waitress was a middle-aged woman with heavy makeup and a brisk manner. But there was something motherly in her concern for Val.

"Boyfriend?" At first Val didn't understand what she meant. "I don't have any boyfriend."

"Sure you do. That character who met you in here yesterday." Val noticed the tone of disapproval on the word *character*. She looked down at her coke.

"He's not my boyfriend."

"You looked pretty thick to me."

"Well, we weren't," Val replied. "Not in *that* way. He's just a friend of mine."

"Oh," said the older woman knowingly. She walked away chuckling.

Val had tried to keep from showing her irritation at the waitress's appraisal of Paul. *That's the way with Boomers. Just because he has long hair, she had to put him down. She didn't know or even care that he is a beautiful person who has more understanding than anyone else I've ever talked to.* Val didn't care what the waitress or anyone else thought about Paul. He was a tremendous individual, and nobody was going to tell her whether or not she should be with him.

Not that I'll ever get the chance, she told herself sadly. He hadn't said anything about seeing her again. True, he hinted at it, but that didn't mean anything with a person like him. He boasted that he never did anything unless he felt like it. He'd proved it by leaving when his family and the people at school started bugging him.

That's why he's neat. I'm so trapped in that horrible mess at home and can't do a thing about it. When she thought about her dad and mom, her anger flared up. *They only think about themselves, they don't care anything about me.* And if she should come to their minds, they tried to figure out what miserable task they could make her do.

Paul wouldn't put up with that kind of treatment. He had plenty of trouble at home, but he hadn't let it get him uptight. He had dropped out of school. He hadn't even been home for two years. He was independent. He did exactly what he wanted to.

Val didn't know whether she really wanted to go that far or not. She wanted to get an education, and she did love her parents in spite of the fact that they didn't care anything about her. Only she wasn't going to have them on her back all the time. If they kept bugging her, she'd have to do something about it. A person was entitled to be free.

At last, reluctantly, she decided Paul wasn't going to come around. She went to the counter, paid for her coke, and trudged out into the bleak, late winter afternoon. Rain clouds hung in the west, hiding the peaks of the distant mountains, and the rising wind was rattling the naked branches of the aspen.

Cars were rushing along the street, hurrying their passengers home to dinner. Val eyed them hopefully. Paul hadn't come into the café, but he might drive by before she got home. Even as the thought came, she realized how foolish it was. A guy like him would be in Denver or Colorado Springs or Salt Lake City. *He goes wherever he feels like going. He's completely free!*

She wondered what it would be like to go around with someone like him. It would be exciting, there was no doubt of that. No more being bored with life. That night she dreamed about life with Paul, and in her dream she had more fun than she ever had in real life.

It was several days before Val saw Paul again. She had begun to think he had left town and wouldn't be back when she saw his car driving up the street early in the evening. The peace sign on the back of his car seemed to wave to her. A new exhilaration took hold of her. He was looking for her. That was the only reason he would be driving along her street.

She hadn't planned to go out that evening, but when she saw Paul's car, she decided to make a trip to the library. Her parents were more likely to let her go to the library than any other place during the week. She used it frequently.

As she left the house after dinner, she saw his car a quarter of a block ahead. Her pace quickened and her hand came up quickly to wave at him. But that was foolish, she told herself. In the growing darkness he would never see her.

Paul turned at the next corner. She was sure he was heading in the direction of the café where they had met. Her first reaction was to go there, too, but that wouldn't do any good. It would take her at least twenty minutes to walk that far. Long before she got there, he would have checked out the café and given up on it. It was better to go on to the library. That might be one of the places he would look if he wanted to find her.

She went to the library solely because of Paul, but she did have plenty of studying to keep her busy until closing time. She didn't stay that long, however. If he should come back looking for her, a few extra minutes would give them more time to be together. Anyway, she was so excited she couldn't keep her mind on her studying.

She walked little more than a block when she saw a pair of headlights turn from the street she lived on and move slowly in the direction of the library. Her pulse quickened.

It was Paul! It had to be! She didn't know how she knew that, but she did! And he was going to stop and pick her up.

In two or three minutes that familiar vehicle swung over to the curb and stopped beside her. The driver lowered the window on the passenger's side.

"Hi, there! Want a ride?"

Val's heart raced! He had come back! Out of all the girls he knew, he had chosen her and had come back to find her! She didn't see how she could possibly have been so lucky.

Her pulse skipped as she went over to his car.

"Hi," she said, managing a bright smile.

"Hop in, kid. I'd like to talk to you. Or are you afraid your parents will get on your back if you're seen with me?"

"They don't tell me what to do." She went to the other side of the car and got in.

"That's right, baby. Don't let anybody shove you around. That's the law of my life."

"I know."

"As far as I'm concerned, it ought to be the golden rule."

She moved a little closer to him, hoping he would put his arm about her. "I'm glad to see you. I was beginning to think you'd taken off without saying goodbye."

"I may be going one of these days, but right now I've decided I can't leave you for very long. You've gotten under my skin." He put his arm around her and drew her close.

Val momentarily was uncertain if Paul was being sincere. Could she mean so much to him already? But she wanted so desperately to believe him that she closed her mind to anything else. There was no reason why he wouldn't want to keep on seeing her. After all, he had come back.

How could I be so lucky as to have a guy like Paul interested in me? She had been feeling sorry for herself, but now her self-pity had vanished, wiped away in the length of time it took her to walk to his car and get in.

It didn't matter anymore how her parents treated her. All she cared about was Paul and the fact that he liked her. She wasn't even concerned about getting home late. Her mother would be mad and storm around and maybe ground her for a few days, but Val was willing to risk it. Paul, however, insisted that he get her home early.

"As long as you're livin' at home," he said, "you'd better get in when you're supposed to. If you don't, your parents'll ground you and we won't get to see each other as often as we want to."

Her spirits soared even higher than before. She knew Paul well enough to know he wouldn't have said that if he didn't plan on coming back to see her – often.

He liked her. He really liked her!

* * *

At the church youth group meeting, Val's older brother, Bill, asked the group to pray for her.

"We have been," one of the girls said. "A group of us have agreed to pray for her every night."

He smiled. "Thanks. I really needed that. She keeps our whole family guessing."

"Have you tried to invite her to some of our meetings?"

"Do you know Val?" he countered.

"Only when I see her."

"She's one person you don't get to go anywhere unless she wants to. She won't listen to anyone!"

CHAPTER 4

VAL GETS DROPPED

During the next several weeks Val Anderson counted the days by her dates with Paul Keller. She was lifted up to a breathless, never-never land when she was with him and plunged into despondency when he didn't come by. At times she was sure he would be hers for always, that he would finally get a job and stay in Rock Point until she was out of school, and they could be married.

True, he had never said anything about marriage. He hadn't even told her he loved her, but she was sure he must. At least he seemed to enjoy being with her.

When she hadn't seen him for several days, which was often, she was afraid something had happened to him or he had grown tired of her and moved on. He didn't make any promises to her. He didn't even tell her when she would see him again – if ever. He might come driving along in his old car the day after they had been together, or it might be a week later. Somehow, he seemed to know just where she was. And whenever he did come, he expected her to go with him.

Not that she didn't want to. Just seeing him pull up to the curb in his car as she was walking to school was enough to send her spirits soaring. She would have gone with him at any time if she was free to do as she pleased. But there was still the problem of her parents and Bill. They didn't want her to date at all, let alone at Paul's weird hours. Paul was careful not to appear at the Anderson home when Bill and her parents were there.

"I can't go with you when it's so late, Paul," she told him reluctantly when he showed up on the front porch at 10:45 one night when both her parents were late getting home. "You know what my parents would say if I did."

"Sneak out after they're in bed."

"Oh, I couldn't do that."

"You could if you want to be with me," he retorted. "It's no big deal. Just be quiet leaving and coming back, and they'll never know you're gone."

She wished she could, but she knew better than to try. If her parents didn't hear her, Bill was sure to. His room was right next to hers. A few months before she could have trusted Bill to keep quiet about it. They stood together then. But now that he was on that religious kick, she couldn't depend on him. If he knew she was sneaking out, maybe he'd feel like it was his duty to tell their parents, and then she'd be in big trouble.

"I wouldn't dare," she told Paul.

"Then you didn't mean what you said about liking me."

"Don't say that! You know I'd do anything for you!"

"Except slip out for a few minutes so we could talk."

She tried hard to make him understand. Finally, he quit pleading with her.

"Okay, if that's the way it is, I suppose that's the way it's got to be. But I can tell you right now that I don't like it. Any girl of mine has got to want to be with me enough to take a few chances."

The next two or three nights Val cried herself to sleep. She didn't think Paul would ever come back, but he did. After that incident, he only came around as she was walking to school or as she was coming home in the afternoon. There would be a few minutes together, talking the way they had before, but then Paul would let her out, and his car would screech away.

It was disturbing to Val. Something had happened between them. There was a barrier blocking their friendship. It bothered her so much that she decided to tell Paul how she felt about him and how much she missed him. She had worked out how she would bring up the subject and what she would say. But the talk didn't turn out the way she wanted it to.

"I've lain awake for the longest time the last three or four nights," she began.

He glanced at her warily. "And what's that to me?" he demanded.

She was shaken by his indifference. "It's been so long since we've been together for a whole evening–" Even though she had gone that far with her plan to talk to him, she could not force herself to put her fears into words.

Paul's grip on the wheel tightened and his features grew hard.

"There's one thing we've got to get straight, Val," he said. "You know I don't like being pushed around. We're good friends now. That's got to be enough. Let's leave it that way. I don't answer to anybody, not even a cute little gal like you."

Val's heart sank.

"I wasn't trying to get you to answer to me," she pleaded. "Honest!" She would die if she said or did something to cause him to dump her and she didn't get to see him anymore. "It's just that we're such good friends and I like being with you so much it bothers me when we don't get to be together for so long, that's all. I don't want you to do anything you don't want to."

His grin lightened her fears.

"That's different. I like being with you, too, but I don't want to be tied down by you or anyone else. If anyone tries to shove me into their tight little mold, I bug out of there fast. That's one thing I can't stand!"

She settled back in the seat uneasily. Paul said he liked her a lot. *I wonder if he means it? Sometimes, I think it's all over and I'll never see him again. But he's the only one I have. Dad is only interested in his work and his bottle, and mom doesn't care about anything as long as there is a bingo party for her to go to. Maybe Bill is concerned about me – but he's too concerned. He's so religious, he's a pain to everyone around him.*

All she had left was Paul. She had to keep seeing him! Life wouldn't be worth living if he wasn't around.

For several weeks Val was increasingly afraid that Paul would be leaving, that with each visit maybe she was seeing him for the last time. She had the impression that he was getting tired of her. Little things he said made her feel she was no longer as important to him as she once was.

Val had no sure indication he was going to stop seeing her. The last time they were together Paul acted no different than he had on other occasions. Only that ended it. He didn't come around anymore.

At first, she tried to make herself believe it hadn't happened, that he had taken one of his frequent trips out of town and would be back any time to take up where they had left off. She kept looking for him on the way to school in the morning and when she walked home at night, but there was no sign of the old familiar car with its peace sign on the back. She couldn't accept the fact that he had gone.

A terrible emptiness took hold of Val the day she finally realized he wouldn't be coming around to see her anymore. It had happened – Paul had tired of her. The sun lost its brilliance for Val, and home became more intolerable than ever. School, too, was a bore.

Bill saw the change that had come over her and asked about it. At first, she tried to ignore him, but he kept after her.

"What's wrong, Val?" he questioned when they were home alone on one of their mother's bingo nights.

"Nothing."

"Don't try to tell me that. I know better. What is it?"

"Why do you think anything is wrong?"

"You're not yourself, Val. What's bothering you?"

"Why don't *you* tell *me* what it is?" she exploded. "Then we'll both know."

"I haven't lived around you all these years without learning something about you. You've been uptight for a week. What's up?"

"There's nothing wrong with me!" she retorted. "There's nothing wrong! How many times do I have to tell you that?"

His eyes narrowed. "Maybe there isn't, but you sure don't act like it."

She didn't like lying to Bill. *I wish I could tell him about Paul, but he wouldn't understand.*

The next week Val kept looking for Paul every time

she went to school or walked home. She even went to the café where they first met and sat for half an hour, dawdling over a coke, hoping he would come in and walk over to her table.

She wanted to ask somebody in the greasy, little eating place if they had seen Paul the last few days, but that would be even worse than talking to Bill, she decided. *The people who work here are so stupid and prejudiced they can't stand him. Even if they knew, they probably wouldn't tell me anything about him.*

At first, she was afraid Paul had tired of her, but as the days went on, she made herself believe there was another reason. *He must have gotten sick,* she told herself. *That has to be the reason. We liked each other too much for him to go away without telling me and saying goodbye.*

He had never talked much about his parents, and she hadn't asked about them. Now she wished she had. If she knew where they were and how to get in touch with them, she'd have called or written to see if they knew where he was.

The more she thought about it, the more sure she was that he was in a hospital, sick and all alone. *The doctors wouldn't even know who to get in touch with if he is. He'd just lie there as though no one else in the whole world cared anything about him.*

She thought about calling the hospitals in Rock Point to see if they had anyone there fitting his description. Once she even looked up a hospital number and started to call before she changed her mind. *If I start calling around, someone will find out about me and Paul and tell my parents or Bill, and I'd be in for it with them.* All she could do was wait and worry.

She flunked another math test during that period of uncertainty, but she didn't really care. She didn't care about anything. How could she? There was only one person in the world who meant anything to her and he had dropped out of her life. For all she knew, he might be dead!

Val left school one afternoon following an interview with the math teacher and walked home. Some friends invited her home with them, but she lied, telling them her parents had grounded her for a month. Val didn't want to be with anyone.

She had walked only two blocks when she saw a familiar car. She recognized the peace sign on the back and her pulse raced. There wasn't another car like that one in Colorado!

Paul was all right! Relief flooded over her. *He must have been out of town for a while and now he's driving by the school to look for me.* She started walking faster, a smile lighting her face.

She expected him to come around the block again in a few minutes and pick her up. She knew what she was going to say to him. She wasn't going to get mad and blast him for not coming to see her. If she did, he would be sure she was trying to make him do something, and he didn't want anybody to tell him what to do. Not even her.

She walked rapidly most of the next block and when he didn't come by, she stopped on the street corner and waited, thinking he would come that way in a few minutes. She was still standing there when Bill's car pulled up at the curb and stopped.

"Hi, Val!" he called out.

She groaned inwardly. He would have to come along right then and ruin everything!

"Hop in. I'll give you a lift."

Reluctantly she went out to the car and got in.

CHAPTER 5

"IT'S ALL BILL'S FAULT"

Riding home with Bill, Val looked desperately for Paul's brilliantly decorated car. If only Bill hadn't come along when he did, she would be with Paul by this time. He must have been looking for her, or he wouldn't have been driving up and down the streets around the school. She had to see him.

She hadn't realized she was so obvious in staring up and down the street at each intersection, but Bill noticed.

"Who're you looking for? Somebody I know?"

He meant it as a joke, but she didn't take it that way. Embarrassment darkened her cheeks. "Can't I ride home with you without having you give me the third degree?"

"I thought I could help you look for him, that's all."

"If I want your help, I'll ask for it."

"You don't know how sharp my eyes are. Give me a clue as to who he is, and I'll see him for you."

She bristled. "If I'd known you wouldn't mind your own business, I'd have walked."

When he saw her anger, his voice softened. "Don't get uptight, Val. I was just teasing you."

She looked out the window and said nothing.

"Hey, I said I was sorry."

"I didn't hear you."

"That's what I meant, anyway."

She pulled herself up. "As far as I'm concerned," she retorted, "you can keep your remarks to yourself. They're not very funny."

"Okay. Okay." He gestured his frustration. "Forget I said anything."

The instant he spoke, Val was sorry she had been so sharp with him. Bill had only wanted to be nice and offer her a ride home. He didn't know anything about Paul so he couldn't have known he had kept Val from meeting him just now. Val felt exasperated and helpless.

Neither of them spoke the rest of the way home.

At the dinner table an hour and a half later, Val announced that she had to go to the library again that evening. She made the announcement defensively, as though she expected them to give her some opposition.

"Again?" her mother asked, suspicion entering her voice, "you were there three nights last week."

"Can I help it we keep getting outside reading assignments? You want me to get good grades, don't you?"

"You know we do," her mother replied.

"Then I've got to go to the library tonight." That much was true. She did have to get out of the house and give Paul a chance to find her.

"I'm going uptown for a while this evening, Val. I'll give you a ride," Bill volunteered, hoping to win her forgiveness.

Ordinarily she would have welcomed it but not now. If she rode to the library and back, she would be sure to miss Paul. It was almost as though Bill knew about her friend and was trying to keep her from him.

"No, thank you," she said coldly.

Bill couldn't understand that. "I've never known you to turn down a ride before. Are you still mad about this afternoon?"

"Now, Val," her mother broke in, "that's no way for you to talk to your brother. He's kind enough to offer you a ride. The least you can do is to take it."

Val's eyes flashed. "I don't know why you're so concerned about me all of a sudden," she told him. "A couple of weeks ago you wouldn't take me anywhere. Now you want to haul me around all the time. I don't get it!"

"I've decided to be nicer to you."

"Great! I suppose I'm helping you earn your brownie points!"

"That's right," he grinned. "If I'm nice to you three days in a row, I get a gold star on my chart."

Bill laughed, but he thought back to the last youth meeting at church. He had asked Danny Orlis what the best way was of making Jesus Christ real to Val and his parents.

"If you want your family to become interested in the Lord," Danny said, "you can't just use words."

"That's good," replied Bill. "I'm not always so good at explaining things."

"They've got to see Jesus Christ in your life," Danny continued. "They've got to see that your love for Him is making a difference in the way you act toward them. If you don't, you'll never get through to them."

Bill Anderson thought over those words. He had always believed he treated Val and his parents okay, and the reason they weren't interested in committing their lives to Jesus Christ was because they were too involved in their escapes. After listening to Danny, however, Bill began to see that his own behavior was involved too. He really couldn't expect them to want to become believers unless they could see a new reality in his own life. They discounted his explanations because there was very little change in his relationship with them. At that moment, Bill had decided he must let Christ show through his life so that Val and his parents would *know* he was different.

But now his sister hadn't reacted the way he thought she would. Bill had wanted to be helpful, but instead Val was disturbed by his offer of a ride to the library. He felt completely baffled.

She went into the other room and got her coat. She didn't know how she would manage it, but she was going to escape from the house without having to ride to the library with Bill and risk having him ruin her relationship with Paul. She was at the back door and would have been gone in a few seconds, but her dad saw her.

"Where are you going, Val?" he asked accusingly.

She turned to face him. "I've got some studying to do at the library."

"Is Bill going to take you?"

"No, he isn't going to take me!" she exploded. "I'm quite capable of getting to the library and back by myself."

He had been drinking that evening, and her sudden anger infuriated him. "Just for that, young lady, you're going to stay home tonight!"

She stared incredulously at him.

"What have I done now?"

"If you don't know, I shouldn't have to tell you. You've turned that temper of yours loose on me once too often tonight. I'm not taking any more of it. Get to your room and stay there until you can apologize and learn to keep a civil tongue in your head!"

"But Dad!" He couldn't do that to her! Paul had been driving around since after school looking for her. If he didn't see her soon, he might think she didn't care about him. He might quit looking for her. If that happened, she didn't even want to live!

"Don't you talk back to me!" He took a step toward her, his flushed face harsh with anger. "You may think you're a big girl now, but you're not too big for a good strapping. One more crack out of you and I'll use my belt on you! Understand?"

Tears flooded her eyes and trailed down her cheeks. Paul was out there driving up and down the streets looking for her, but there was no use in her trying to argue with her dad. When he'd been drinking and got mad at her, there was nothing anyone could say to change his mind. In that mood he just might hit her. It wouldn't be the first time!

"What do you expect?" she demanded. "You treat me like a baby!"

With that she fled to her room and slammed the door, almost running into her brother as she did so. Bill stared after her in bewilderment. When Danny had talked about showing love to the members of his family, Bill thought it would be like magic. His parents and Val would immediately notice the change and try to understand what caused it. But instead, he had caused a family dispute. *I just don't get it,* he thought.

Val cried herself to sleep that night. Once or twice, she woke up and lay awake for a long while thinking about Paul. *I've lost him now,* she told herself. *And it's all Bill's fault!*

The next morning on the way to school she thought she saw her friend's car, but she wasn't sure. She only glimpsed a car that careened around the corner and sped away.

Her doubts came rushing back – doubts about Paul and his feeling toward her. *Maybe he is tired of me. Maybe he has been cruising around looking for another girl and hadn't been wanting to see me at all.*

But that couldn't be. Paul still had her ring and was wearing it on a chain around his neck. He had given her the charm he had been wearing and told her that he would give the ring back to her if he got tired of having her as his girlfriend. And he had never lied to her – well, almost never. He wouldn't lie about anything so important. And she still had the charm, and he still had her ring, so there had to be some other reason – like not being able to find her on the way home from school.

Her dad had been more angry than usual about the disagreement they had, and he made her stay home for a while. It was not until Friday evening that Val was allowed to go out. He hesitated for a moment when she asked about going to a movie, and she was sure he was going to refuse again. Surprisingly, he said yes.

"Only I want you home right afterward. Understand?"

She nodded.

Val was half a block from the theater when she saw a familiar figure standing at the ticket booth. Paul! He was in Rock Point after all! She was about to call out his name when she saw that he was not alone. A tall, long-haired blonde was with him, clinging possessively to his arm.

Val didn't go to the movie that night. She could not bring herself to go into that building, knowing some other girl was sitting beside Paul.

Val turned and stumbled blindly away. She didn't know how many blocks she walked or where she went. She had lost Paul to someone else. She would never be his girl again. A terrible heaviness swept over her.

She walked longer than she realized when she finally turned wearily toward home. Her mother was there, back from her weekly bingo party, and her dad was sitting in the living room waiting for her.

The explosion that night was worse than the one earlier in the week. All of her dad's resentment and frustration boiled out. She would have explained, but how could she make them understand? They would be more furious than ever if they found out about Paul. And right then she was too miserable to hear much more.

"There–there was a double feature," she lied defensively.

"Don't lie to me again!" Her dad's voice thundered through the house. "I checked! Now I want an explanation, and I want it fast! Who were you with and where have you been at this hour?"

"I–I haven't been with anybody. I was just walking around."

He wouldn't believe that either. He stormed at her and threatened to use his belt on her if she didn't tell the truth and finally ordered her to her room.

"And I want you to know you're not going anywhere after supper until we get this thing straightened out. Understand?"

"I–I have told you the truth," she protested tearfully.

"Go to your room, Valerie!" he snapped, "or I'll lose my temper and give you the thrashing you ought to have!"

She went to her bedroom and locked the door. She wasn't going to have her mother coming in and slobbering all over her, telling her how sorry she was Val hadn't told them the truth.

The distraught girl stood at the window looking out into the darkness. *I don't have to stay here and take that kind of guff,* she told herself. *Paul kept telling me I was a fool not to split.*

And why shouldn't she? The only person who cared anything about her was gone from her life. There was no reason for her to stick around anymore!

She came back to her bed and sat down on the edge. If she did leave, she would have to have some money. At least enough to keep her going until she found a job. At first that seemed to be an insurmountable obstacle. Then she remembered she had money in the bank. There were birthday and Christmas gifts from her grandparents and the few dollars she had saved by babysitting. She'd been saving it for college.

That night she worked it all out in detail. She would get a few of her things together in an old suitcase and sneak it outside where she'd hide it until she was ready. Then she'd go down to the bank and close out her savings account. The tellers were at the windows for an hour every Saturday morning. Once she had her savings she'd pick up her suitcase and take off for Denver. She'd get a job there and wouldn't have to worry about her dad and mom ordering her around. She'd show them exactly how she felt about them.

A fierce excitement gripped her.

CHAPTER 6

A MISSING PERSON

The following morning Val was up an hour before anyone else. She packed a few clothes in the old suitcase from her closet and smuggled it out to the garage where she hid it behind a pile of old boards. Choosing the clothes to pack wasn't easy. She didn't like leaving some of her nicest things at home, but she couldn't take everything with her. Besides, it wouldn't really matter what she had along. Even though she wouldn't be with Paul, she had already decided she wanted to live the way he and his friends lived. She wouldn't have any use for nice clothes.

At the thought of Paul, the dull ache came back to rest heavily on her heart once more. If she had had the courage to drop out of school and take off with him, they might still be together. Thinking back, she could see that he had hinted often enough at it. But she had allowed her parents and Bill to stand in the way. She didn't blame him for running out on her. She had given him second or third place in her life. Maybe they would meet each other sometime, and if he saw that she had followed his advice and taken off, he might ask her to go out with him. She wouldn't miss another chance. She was sure of that.

It helped a bit to daydream that way, but she knew it would never come true. She should have known that a neat guy like Paul wouldn't be satisfied with her very long. He would want an older, more sophisticated woman.

Back in the house again, she waited impatiently for an opportunity to leave without being found out. *I've got to play it carefully or I'll be discovered, and then things would really be messed up. I must act as though there's nothing wrong, that I'm the same person I was yesterday.*

Val was almost cheerful as she helped with the breakfast dishes. Doing the housework wasn't so bad when she knew this was the last time she would have to do it. She thought, *I better not act too happy.* After all, she was supposed to be grounded. She shouldn't be smiling as though everything was okay.

She was almost sorry for her mom and the rest of the family. They had to stay in their grubby little corner of the world with nothing to look forward to.

But not me! I'm breaking out of it! They weren't going to hammer her into the same kind of a miserable existence. She was going to run her own life.

She'd get out and see the world and have a ball. She might come home after a few years, when she was old enough so her parents couldn't get their hooks into her again. Maybe they would treat her better when they saw that they couldn't dictate everything she did or didn't do.

Half the morning was gone before she had a chance to get away from her mother.

Val expected to be seen getting the suitcase from the garage. She was so exposed leaving during the daytime that she was sure she would be caught. She prepared herself to be discovered, deciding her plan was stupid. *I'm so helpless I can't even get out of the house without being seen.*

Events went better than she expected. Her mother was on her phone finding out about the day's bingo party. Bill had already left for work. Val suspected that her dad was probably still in bed; she hadn't seen him all morning. So nobody noticed Val as she left the garage, crossed the back lawn, and made her way up the alley to the end of the block.

Resentment and anger flooded over her. If they had only treated her normally, like people did who really loved their daughters, she wouldn't be running away! But her parents weren't like other kids' parents. They didn't think anything of her. They'd be glad when she was gone. They wouldn't have to worry about when she would be in or who she was with.

Well, if that was what they wanted, she'd give it

to them. She was going to run her own life! Let them do what they pleased, and she'd do the same!

It was a long walk to the bus station on the fringe of the business district, and the suitcase was heavy. Several times she had to stop and rest. By the time she reached her destination and put the bag in a locker, she wished she had left half the stuff at home.

From the bus depot she went to the bank, closed out her account, and returned to the station to buy a ticket to Cheyenne. Once that was done, she counted her money again. She had a little more than three hundred dollars in cash. That was more money than she had ever had at one time before. She didn't know for sure how long three hundred dollars would last. *I'll have to get a job soon,* she decided.

Val got on the bus to Cheyenne, but she had no intention of going there. She only went to the first stop north of Rock Point. There she got off, cashed in her ticket, and bought another to Denver. It was a trick she had seen in a detective movie on TV. If her parents did try to follow her, that might give them a little trouble. It might even throw them off completely.

She had been to Denver more times than she could count and thought she knew the city well, but she had never gone there alone. When she got off the bus in midafternoon, she was trembling inside. Where would she go? What would she do now? Somehow, she hadn't thought getting away on her own could be like this.

Val's consternation must have been visible. A gray-haired woman who had been on the same bus came over to her.

"What's the matter, dear?"

Val faced her defensively. "Nothing."

"Is someone supposed to meet you?"

She shook her head quickly, hoping to get rid of the woman as quickly as possible.

"Oh, no, there isn't anyone to meet me. I–I live here."

"My husband is coming to pick me up. Could we take you to your home?"

Confusion filled Val's eyes. Why didn't the woman go away and leave her alone? Why did she have to keep sticking her nose into something that wasn't any of her business?

"I'll just take a bus home, thank you."

The kind questioner was still not satisfied with Val's answers, but she didn't quite know what to do.

"If there is anything I can do–"

"Oh, no. No, thanks!" She looked at her watch. "I'd better hurry or I'll miss my bus!"

She left the station by a side door and hurried up the street. She wanted to look back to see if the woman was watching her, but she dared not. She didn't want to make her any more suspicious than she was already.

* * *

The Andersons were not particularly disturbed by Val's absence Saturday morning. She sometimes went out on Saturday, loafing around in the stores uptown with friends or going to someone's house to study or goof around playing music. Noon came and they were still not too disturbed.

"I don't like the way that girl's acting lately," her dad said, still smarting from the scene the night before. "We've got to crack down on that kid, or we're going to have a real problem on our hands. She doesn't think she has to pay attention to anything I say."

"She probably went to see one of her friends," her mother replied defensively. "She's got to get out of the house once in a while."

"I know that, but she can be here for meals and act as though the rest of us count for something. She's the queen bee as far as she's concerned. She's got to get rid of that idea or she won't be going anywhere. I'll see to that."

"Don't be too hard on her."

"There you go, sticking up for her. I'm going to have a talk with her, just the same. She's got to let us know where she's going and who she's with and when she'll be back, or I'll see that she stays home all the time. That's a promise!"

His wife did not reply. If she said what she was thinking, she decided, they would only have another argument. There had been enough of those lately. It seemed to her they were fighting all the time.

Bill came home a few minutes later and asked about his sister. There was a party at church he wanted to take her to that night if he could talk their dad into relenting a little.

"She hasn't come home for dinner yet," Mr. Anderson snarled.

"Where'd she go?"

"Where does she usually go?"

"She's still upset about the way you yelled at her last night," his wife said.

"I should have started yelling earlier and louder, if you ask me."

Irene Anderson got her phone and called several of Val's best friends. She knew she had to get her daughter home, or there'd be another big scene. But none of Val's friends had seen her. For the first time, Irene was concerned. She went back to the living room and sat down wearily.

"I'm worried about Val, Bart," she said. "None of the girls have seen her all day."

"There's nothing to be so upset about. She's just trying to scare us, that's all. I tell you, we've got to crack down on that kid or she's going to rule the roost around here! We can't let her go on this way."

"The girls all told me Valerie has been acting strange the last few days. They've been wondering what's wrong with her. She hasn't wanted to have anything to do with any of them."

When the middle of the afternoon came and she

still had not come home, Barton Anderson became as concerned as his wife. He paced the floor incessantly and once or twice got in the car and drove down by the library and some teenage hangouts. But there was no sign of her.

Several hours later he called the hospital and the police to see if they knew anything about her. The sergeant at the police desk was cold and impersonal.

"If she's still gone Monday, you can come in and file a missing persons' report if you want to."

"Oh, that won't be necessary," Bart retorted quickly. "We're sure she's around town somewhere."

"Well, Mr. Anderson, I hope so. If you decide you need our help, you'll have to come in to fill out the forms. Bring a copy of the latest picture you have of her."

When Bart hung up, his wife walked over to him, fear on her face. "She hasn't been arrested, has she?"

He shook his head. For the first time in months, he thought about his wife's feelings. He didn't want to tell her everything the sergeant said because he didn't want her to get more upset than she already was.

Until right then he hadn't been too disturbed about their daughter not being at home. He had been uneasy, but he hadn't seriously believed that she might be gone. He had been sure she was in town with one of her friends, sulking somewhere because he got after her for staying out late and lying to them. Now, however, he was deeply concerned. All sorts of things could happen to a girl her age. He started for the door again.

"I think I'll go out and look for her again."

His wife stopped him with a warning. "You stay away from that tavern!"

Bart whirled and faced his wife, saying bitterly, "I should have expected you to make a crack like that!"

"That's where you usually go!"

"At least I've got sense enough not to waste my life playing bingo!"

Their usual hostility gripped them, and they were about to continue when Bill came in. Bart Anderson left, slamming the door as his final blow in the argument.

Bill heard most of what they said but ignored it. He didn't see how they could fight when Val was gone, and nobody knew where. She must have left home before ten o'clock that morning, and now it was almost seven and still there was no word from her.

He didn't think she would actually run away, even though there had been trouble with the parents. They had been on her back about being out late the night before, and she'd been mad about it. Still, he didn't think she was stupid enough to leave home. She did some dumb things once in a while, but he knew her well enough to be positive she wouldn't want to hurt herself and their parents and everyone else. More likely she was staying away to get back at them.

What his mother had said about Val's friends

thinking she had been upset lately bothered him more than anything else. She had seemed that way to him too. At times she didn't act like herself at all.

But that wasn't all that bothered him. He had been hearing other things about her. Some of the guys told him they'd seen her with some weirdo who was hanging around town. Bill had been wanting to talk to her about the character but hadn't had much of a chance. Every time he got on the subject, she turned him off.

By eight o'clock Bill had telephoned Del and three other Christian guys, asking them to pray for his sister. Then he went to his room where he, too, got down on his knees.

CHAPTER 7

A PLACE TO STAY

Val Anderson was glad she left home now that she was gone. Everything had gone wrong back in Rock Point the last few months. First Paul had thrown her over for another girl. Then her parents had been impossible. They treated her like a little girl and didn't give her credit for knowing anything or doing anything right. They weren't satisfied unless they dictated every move she made. And Bill was terrible since he had become so religious. Whenever she gave him an opening, he started preaching to her.

But now she was through with all of them: Paul, her parents, and her religious brother. She never wanted to see any of them again. She was going to make a life for herself. She was never going to have anyone else tell her what to do.

However, as the shadows of the towering hills west of Denver lengthened and night began to wrap the city in gloom, her anger gave way to fear. She had planned exactly what she would do after leaving the bus station. She made her way to one of the better hotels in the business district and asked about a room. Her heart sank when she heard the price.

She had hoped her three hundred dollars would last her at least two weeks. But she soon learned that she would not be able to stay in the sort of place she planned. She tried two or three other hotels that looked a little cheaper, but the answer was the same. Her money wouldn't last more than a few days if she had to rent a hotel room and start paying for her meals.

Gradually she drifted into a less desirable part of the downtown area in search of a cheaper place to stay. After a time, she discovered a couple of hotels that looked as though they would be cheaper, but there were only elderly men in the lobbies, and she was afraid to go in. So she moved on.

Now that it was getting darker, her fright began to build. She wouldn't be able to stay on the streets for another half hour, that was for sure. Already she was afraid to walk past some of the alleys. She tightened her grip on her suitcase and began to walk faster. At the corner she spotted a hamburger stand and went in for a coke, taking the only available seat at the counter.

She hadn't been there more than a minute or two when the girl sitting next to her spoke. "Hi, babes."

Val started nervously, and she turned her head quickly in the direction of the husky voice.

"Don't get uptight. I just want to be friendly."

She studied the older girl curiously. She was thin and pinch-faced, looking almost old enough to be Val's mother. Yet it was obvious that she was in her early twenties.

"The name's Betty."

"I'm Val. Valerie Anderson."

Betty was wearing a thin, cotton shirt and frazzled jeans that offered little protection against the cold mountain air. Her hair was scraggly and uncombed, as though she no longer cared. For an instant, Val was repulsed by her, but her smile was bright and friendly.

"You're new in town," Betty said, her long, bony fingers taking hold of Val's arm reassuringly. She seemed aware that Val had arrived only hours before.

"How do you know?"

Betty laughed without humor. "How do I know a lot of things? I've been around, baby. I've been around." Her voice hardened. "What are you doing here? Why did you come to Denver?"

Val had no immediate reply. It was hard for her to find words to tell a stranger why she had left home and come to Denver. She wouldn't understand.

"You don't have to answer," the other girl said quickly. "You're here. The reason you came is your business."

Val smiled gratefully.

"Tell me," Betty continued, "have you got a place to stay?"

Val shook her head. She not only didn't have a place to stay, but she also had no idea how she would go about finding one she could afford.

The older girl seemed to understand more than Val thought she would. She asked no more questions but repeated her invitation.

"You can come up to my place if you want to," she said. "It's not much, but it's a place to stay."

She studied Betty's deep-set eyes curiously, trying to decide if it would be all right for her to go with her. There was a disturbing hardness in her new friend's eyes and an edge to her voice Val was unable to define. She had to have a place to stay, but she didn't know whether it would be safe for her to go with the older girl or not.

"There are other kids at my place most of the time," Betty went on. "They come and go. But there's room for you. I'll make room if I have to kick somebody else out to do it." She tightened her grip on Val's arm. "You can't wander around this part of town after dark. I'm telling you. It isn't safe!"

Val wasn't sure why she went with Betty. She hadn't wanted to. But what the other girl said about not daring to be on the street in that section of town after dark was true. There were taverns and cheap hotels for men in every block. Already they had started whistling at her and making suggestive remarks. With so little money, though, she could not afford a decent hotel. And she had to have some place to stay.

"I–I guess it'll be all right."

Betty's anger flashed. "If it isn't nice enough for you, your royal highness, you might get the presidential suite at the Brown Palace. I'm sure it would have everything you're accustomed to."

"I–I'm sorry," Val stammered. She had never known anyone who was so quick to explode. Not even Paul. "I didn't mean I was afraid it won't be nice enough for me." She started to cry. "I don't know what I mean."

Instantly Betty softened. "Forget it. We'll go to my place and see if we can whip up something to eat. Okay?"

She nodded.

They crossed the street and turned left in the direction of the building where Betty had an apartment. "I want to warn you, kid. There was quite a bunch at my place when I left, and they were having a blast. I hope they don't shake you up too much." Her eyes narrowed. "But they're my kind. I want you to know that."

At that point Val was too bewildered and upset to care. She went with her new friend to the opposite end of the block, crossed that street, and went back to an alley stairway that led to a second-floor loft where Betty had several rooms.

"This is where we go in," she said. "It's really a dump, but it's out of the weather."

Val shuddered as they started up the dark stairway together. This place was a lot different than her parents' home or that of any of her friends back in Rock Point. But that was all behind her, she told herself. She was going to forget Rock Point ever existed. She was going to be free and run her own life.

"These kids are really kind of freaky," Betty said once more, "but you don't have to worry about them. They're okay."

Val mumbled something. Even as she spoke, however, she wasn't aware of what she said. Her emotions were churning until she was scarcely capable of thinking. At the top of the stairs, she fought against a desire to flee. *What am I getting myself into?* She was afraid to go into the apartment, but she was even more afraid to go back on the street.

Betty opened the door, and they stepped inside. Val turned slowly, staring at a dozen teenagers who were there. The lights were low, and a thick, sweet smoke hung in the air.

Her new friend was studying her reaction. "Well, here we are."

Still Val did not move. She could not. But it seemed that no one was paying attention to her. It was almost as though she hadn't even come into the room.

"Pick a spot and sit down if you can." Betty took

Val's suitcase and walked out of the room. Most of the group seemed indifferent to both Betty and Val.

The smoke was different from anything Val had ever smelled before. Slowly she realized that it was marijuana. She stood motionless, stunned by the realization that she was actually at a weed party, until one of the boys came swaggering over to her. He was several years older than Val, a towering, spindly individual with burning eyes and slow, languid movements. The pupils of his eyes were dilated, and a crooked grin was clamped on his face.

"Hi, there," he said.

She tried to ignore him.

"I said hi."

Still she did not answer. His smile faded.

"What's with you? You sure don't know how to be friendly."

Val was trembling so much she didn't know whether she could speak or not, but she had to say something to him.

"I think your friend over there wants you to come back." She motioned to the girl who was sitting cross-legged on the floor near the blaring speaker, swaying lazily to the music.

"Her?" He laughed. "She's a drag."

"Maybe I'm a drag, too." Val was terrified, but she couldn't let him know it.

"Now, don't be like that," he jeered. "Come on

over and get acquainted. You'll find me sweet and lovable, honey."

She stared at him, repulsed by the expression on his face. Although Val had never been around guys who lacked moral control, she instinctively recognized lust. She backed to the door, helplessly.

"I–" Her mouth was dry and hot.

"I've got some real good grass I've been saving, sweetheart. Until right now, I didn't know why. Now I see it was just for you. Come on, let's sit down and try some Acapulco Gold straight from Mexico. It'll make you forget all your troubles, and you and I can begin to enjoy ourselves. Won't that be nice?"

He reached out to put his arm around her, but she shrank away.

"Leave me alone!" she protested.

"Hey, she's a real touchy one," he teased. "I don't like girls who play hard to get. Come on and be sociable."

Val continued to move backward until she felt the wall behind her. She could no longer retreat.

CHAPTER 8

BETTY'S STORY

Val Anderson glanced wildly about the room. She was about to scream when Betty came back and saw what was happening. The muscles in her thin face tightened, and anger leaped into her eyes. She stormed over to her young guest.

Betty grasped the boy by the arm and spun him to face her. "Knock it off, Gus!" she rasped.

"Now, Betty, don't do that to me. She's a cute kid. The two of us will get along fine. Don't worry about that."

"I said, knock it off! And that's what I mean. Leave her alone!"

Val moved closer to Betty, shrinking back until the older girl was between her and the persistent young man.

"What if I don't leave her alone?" he blustered.

"What are you going to do about it? Are you goin' to call the police?"

She swore at him.

"You know me better than that. I don't have to call the cops to handle a cheap little jerk like you. Leave Val alone or get out of here! You can take your choice!"

"All I want to do is get her turned on to a little weed. That never hurt anybody. You know that."

Betty stepped closer to him. Val didn't think she had ever seen anyone so angry. The older girl's eyes blazed, and her voice was harsh and authoritative. She wasn't as tall as him by half a head, but he retreated, cowed by her forcefulness.

"I'm not havin' you or anyone else in here turning this kid on drugs! You get that now and get it good! If you try it, you'll have to answer to me!"

He shook his head questioningly.

"I don't get it," he mumbled, more to himself than the girls. "You bring her to a weed party, but you don't want her turned on! Why did you bring her here, anyway?"

She grasped his arm just above the elbow and tightened her fingers convulsively until he winced.

"I want you all to hear this!" She was talking so loudly everyone in the room was listening. One of the girls leaned over and shut off the music. "If it hadn't been for some stupid character like you, Gus,

I wouldn't be the kind of a person I am today. That's why I'm not letting you do it to this kid."

"Aw–"

She cut him off. "You listen until I'm through! And this goes for all of you! If anyone here tries to get Val turned on to weed or acid or speed or anything else, I'll take you apart with my bare hands! Understand?"

For an instant or two, all was silent.

Relief flooded over Val. She didn't know how she could have been lucky enough to have someone like Betty take her in. She could easily have fallen in with one of the others. She looked at her friend with new appreciation.

Back in Rock Point, Bill and his friends were praying for her. They got together that Saturday evening, pleading with God to watch over Val and keep her safe. But, of course, she didn't know anything about that.

When the music started once more and Gus went back to his girlfriend, Val turned to Betty. "I'm just causing trouble between you and your friends. I'd better go someplace else."

"You're going to do nothing of the kind. You'll stay right here."

"But your friends will all be mad at you."

"Friends?" She almost spat out the word. "What kind of friends are they? You're not going to leave here. You're staying with me, where you won't have anything to worry about. They won't dare touch anything you eat or drink – or you, either, as long as you're at my place."

"But–"

"Quit wasting my time and shut up! You can't leave this place now, anyway. You wouldn't get two blocks from here at this time of night." Her voice softened. "You don't have to worry. None of these kids will try to cause you any trouble. I may not look like much, but there isn't one of them who dares to cross me." Her eyes flashed. "That's a promise!"

Tears filled the younger girl's eyes.

"You don't know how much I appreciate everything you're doing for me, but I'm just causing trouble."

"You say that again and I'll smack you one!" Betty paused for a time. "This is going to sound strange to you," she continued, "and maybe a little bit stupid, but ever since I first saw you on the street earlier this evening, I've seen myself in you."

"I don't know what you mean."

"I came to Denver a few years ago the same way you did this afternoon. I'd had it up to here with my parents and with school and the boy I'd been dating. I was mad and scared and bewildered when I got here. Now, look at me!" There was loathing in her voice. "If someone had gotten to me when I first hit town, things could have been different for me – so much different than they are now. But I hit the streets and got in with a bunch like Gus and the rest of that bunch of leeches. It wasn't long until I was – like this!"

Val was stunned to hear her talk that way. Betty did look as though she had lived a tough life, but she didn't seem all bad to Val.

"But I don't see–" she began.

The other girl cut her off with a look.

"Look at this. You'll see what I mean!" She thrust out her arm for Val to look at it.

Horror crept into the younger girl's face. She had never actually seen needle tracks before, but she heard enough about them to know with one look at Betty's arm that the older girl was a heroin addict.

Suddenly she saw what Betty was trying to say to her.

"Is–is there anything I can do to help you?" She formed the words hesitantly.

The older girl sat up straight, and her smile flashed bright and hard. "There's nothing you can do for me. The price is too great to get out of it now. I suppose I'll keep on living in this filthy hole until I get an overdose or get so tired of living that I'll take rat poison."

The smile fled from her hard features. "It's too late for me. The bus has already pulled out of the station, and I wasn't on it. But I'm not going to let you get hurt the way I've been. I'm going to keep you from ruining your life if I can!"

* * *

Two days had passed since Val ran away from home. They were two sleepless days and nights for the Anderson family. Bart had been reluctant to file a missing persons' report, but on Monday he did so, and the police in Denver and Cheyenne and the surrounding cities and towns were notified.

"There should be some word of her in a day or two, shouldn't there?" Mr. Anderson asked the officer who took down the information.

"Let's hope so," he replied. "It's a tough world out there for a fourteen-year-old kid, believe me!"

Bart Anderson's throat tightened until he could not speak. He knew, all too well, what the officer was talking about. He himself rubbed shoulders with that kind of life. It was one thing for him to come in contact with it. Thinking his daughter was plunging into the same type of life, or worse, was unthinkable to him.

The family waited hopefully, trying to assure themselves that word would be coming soon that she had been seen somewhere, but that did not happen. She had drawn money out of the bank, they learned, and had bought a bus ticket for Cheyenne, but nobody at that bus station had seen her get off the bus. They were checking at the various stops along the way.

The next day the police learned she had gotten off the bus at the first stop and had bought a ticket back to Denver, cashing in her Cheyenne ticket. But again, they came up against a blank as far as information went.

The terminal at Denver was so large and busy that no one could remember seeing a girl of her description. She might have gotten off between Rock Point and Denver and started hitchhiking, or she could have bought a ticket for some other place. There was no indication of where she had gone or what she had done.

The family was so concerned they could scarcely think of anything else. Twice a day Bill or his dad called the police station. The answer was always the same, however. They had no firm report on her. One afternoon, Bill stopped at the station.

"We had word earlier today that the police in Omaha are holding a girl about the age of your sister, Bill," the officer said. "But she didn't quite fit the description we had. While they were checking her out, we contacted your father to verify the color of her hair and eyes. But I talked with Omaha half an hour ago. They said the girl they have has been positively identified as a missing girl from southwestern Indiana."

Bill's face reflected his disappointment.

"I'm sorry," the police officer added.

Bill thanked him and left, the uneasiness continuing to grow in his stomach. He felt so bewildered – so helpless. If only there was something he could do! If only he could help find her!

He and his parents sat around in the living room that evening, looking at each other but not saying very much. After a final call to the police a little after eleven o'clock, they went to bed.

The lights hadn't been off more than fifteen minutes when the doorbell rang.

"Maybe that's Val!" Irene cried.

Bart stumbled to the closet, got his robe, and went to answer the door. Bill and his mother were only a few steps behind him, going into the living room fearfully.

"Bart Anderson?" the officer at the door asked.

"Yes. Have you found our daughter?"

"I'm afraid I don't have very good news for you."

Bill stared at the somber face of the police officer at the door, apprehension sweeping over him.

CHAPTER 9

THE CAR ACCIDENT

The Anderson family stared at the police officer.

"What is it?" Irene demanded. "What's wrong?"

"There's been an accident," the officer said slowly, "a car accident."

Her eyes widened. "What does that have to do with us?"

"That's what we've got to talk with you about. Has your missing daughter ever been fingerprinted?"

"Val fingerprinted?" Bart broke in, indignation honing his voice. "Of course not!"

"We didn't think she would be, but it is one means of identification. Can you give me the name of her dentist?"

"Certainly, but what's this all about? Have you found Val?"

The officer could avoid them no longer.

"We're not sure yet. We're trying to establish the

identity of a girl who was killed in a car accident on the highway west of town tonight. She and the young man who was driving were both killed instantly. The bodies are badly burned, so identification is difficult."

Their faces went ashen, and Bill pulled in a quick breath. Val killed in an accident? It couldn't be!

"You must be mistaken!" Bart protested, as though voicing denial would help to keep it from being true. "It couldn't be our daughter!"

"I'd like the name of her dentist, please," the young officer said crisply. "We may be able to make a positive identification by her teeth."

Irene went to the desk and got the last card the dentist had given Val, marking her appointment. "But this won't do you any good. He's the dentist whose office was broken into by vandals last month. All the records and X-rays were torn up or burned."

The policeman nodded. "I remember the case. They figured a couple of users broke in looking for drugs, and when they didn't find any, they got so mad they tore things up."

Bart Anderson brought the subject back to their daughter.

"The girl who was killed in that car couldn't be Val. Our daughter's only fourteen. She hasn't shown any interest in boys. I don't think she's ever had a date."

"I'm afraid there are some things about your daughter that you don't know. Her friends tell us she had been seen with the dead boy a number of times in recent weeks."

"I don't believe it," Irene retorted loyally.

Bill didn't want to destroy his mother's hope, but he could not keep anything from her and Dad. They had a right to know.

"That's true, Mom. I've talked with kids who have seen her with this guy. Once or twice, I was sure I saw her in his car."

"You could have been mistaken."

"Maybe, but I don't think so. I know my own sister. I'm almost positive I've seen her with a guy who had a big peace sign on the back of his car."

"That's the boy who had the accident. He must have been going ninety when he went off the road and piled up."

The officer took a small object from his pocket and held it out to Mrs. Anderson. "Have you ever seen this ring?"

The color faded from her cheeks, and her hands trembled. "I–"

"There's an inscription inside. 'To Val from Dad.'"

A shudder swept over Bart's taut frame.

"That's Val's ring, all right. It's the one I gave her for Christmas last year." He paused, turning it thoughtfully between his thumb and forefinger. "Where did you get it?"

"We found it on the body of the dead girl."

Val's mother gasped.

"But–but that's not absolute proof, is it? She could have lost it or given it to somebody or–"

"It isn't absolute proof in itself," the officer answered, "but it is a solid piece of evidence – about the only thing solid we have to go on right now."

He made a notation in his book.

"Can you give me your daughter's height and weight?"

Irene Anderson did so, mechanically.

"How does that fit the height and weight of the girl who was killed?" Bart asked.

"Of course, the weight we have for the dead girl could not be too accurate. She was badly burned. But she is approximately the same height as your daughter." His voice was gentle. "There is nothing conclusive yet, but the evidence does seem to point to the fact that the dead girl could be your missing daughter."

Val's mother swayed and her husband grasped her. He sat her in the living room on the couch. Then he turned his attention to the officer once more.

"Then you really think this dead girl is Valerie?" he asked. For the first time he was shaken.

"It would be a much more certain identification if we had a fingerprint or her dental records for proof, but let's look at what we do have." He outlined the evidence, beginning with the fact that Val had been seen a number of times with the boy who was killed and had been positively identified. "And she was about the same height," he went on, "to say nothing of the ring you have just identified."

"Then you do think it is her, don't you?"

The patrolman shook his head. "We're gathering information right now. We want you to make the decision."

Irene Anderson's eyes were wide and staring. "Would it do any good if we were to go down to the morgue and–"

"I wouldn't advise that, Mrs. Anderson." He spoke quickly. "Take my word for it. There is nothing you can identify."

"The ring is hers," Bart mumbled numbly. "I can vouch for that. I don't like to admit it, but it must be Val."

His wife nodded wordlessly. It didn't seem possible that she could have been killed in the car, but they had to face reality. How could they deny such evidence?

There would be more legalities to be taken care of the next day, but Bart Anderson and his wife were convinced in their own minds that Val had been killed in the car accident.

When the officer was finally gone, Bart whirled on his son suddenly.

"This was all your fault, Bill!" he exploded angrily.

The boy stared at him in disbelief. His dad couldn't mean it, he told himself. He had done everything he could to help Val. He couldn't have been responsible.

"It's all your fault!" he repeated.

"Don't say that!" his wife exclaimed tearfully. "You're only making things worse!"

"But it is Bill's fault!" Bart repeated. "If he hadn't kept preaching at her all the time, she never would have run away. She was always such a good girl until Bill went nuts over religion and tried to make her think she was a terrible sinner unless she hit the sawdust trail the way he did. It's enough to drive anyone out of his mind!"

The sudden attack stunned Bill. He didn't think he had pressed his sister about the claims Jesus Christ had on her life enough to bother her. He had shared his faith with her, but no more than three or four times. It seemed to him she had listened to what he had to say. She hadn't bought it, that was true, but she hadn't gotten mad at him.

There were plenty of other times when he wanted to talk to her about putting her trust in Christ for salvation, but there hadn't been any other opportunities. The last couple of weeks he hadn't even asked her to go to Sunday school or youth meeting with him. He didn't see how he could be the cause of the terrible thing that had happened.

He turned to his dad, nevertheless.

"I don't think I upset her," he said, "but if I did, I'm sorry."

"You're sorry!" All the anger and grief that was in him lashed out. "A lot of good that's going to do! The damage has been done now!"

* * *

Val had not slept well the night of the accident. Betty had been away with some of her friends, and she was in the apartment alone until long after midnight. She got to thinking about her parents and Paul and Bill. For some reason she thought more about her brother than anyone else. She used to get mad at him, but when she thought it over, she realized he really did think a lot of her. He was the one who took her out for a hamburger or a pizza when their parents were gone. And he had been the one who wanted to give her rides to the places she wanted to go. It hadn't been his fault she wanted to walk because she thought Paul Keller was looking for her.

That was a laugh. Paul must have decided he didn't want to have anything to do with her, but she was too blind to see it. He could have found her easily enough if he'd wanted to. He knew where she lived. He even knew the streets she walked on to go to school, and Bill hadn't given her a ride every time she left the house. There was plenty of chance for him to have found her if he'd wanted to.

It hurt to think about it, but she did have to admit now that he had tired of her and didn't want to be around her anymore. He had found somebody else to take her place.

She began to wonder about her parents, too, and if they missed her. She still didn't think they loved her. If they had, they wouldn't have treated her the way they did. But she missed them more than she would let on, even to Betty.

Several kids came home with her friend sometime during the night. They woke her up when they came in and kept her awake for over an hour. But it must have been some party. Everyone else was asleep when she got up at the usual time. She dressed and went into the living room. Before she fixed herself some breakfast, she switched on the television for something to do. She was eating breakfast and half giving her attention to the newscast when the announcer began to report a car accident at Rock Point.

"Two people were killed in a one-car accident shortly after nine o'clock last night on the highway west of Rock Point," the announcer began.

The picture switched to a wrecked car, and Val couldn't believe her eyes. It was Paul's car! Even though it was badly wrecked, she recognized the peace symbol on the back. She would recognize that car anywhere!

She dashed to the TV and turned up the sound, still not completely aware of all that had happened.

"The bodies of the young man and woman in the car were badly burned. The boy has been identified as Paul Keller of upstate New York. The girl is not positively identified yet. Last night, however, the parents of Valerie Anderson, who has been missing since Saturday, told police the ring the victim was wearing belonged to their daughter. It is believed the dead girl was their daughter, Valerie, although investigation is continuing."

The TV was so loud Betty came out, rubbing her head.

"Turn that thing down, Val!" she exclaimed. "You'll have everybody in the place awake!"

Then she saw Val's ashen face and the horror gleaming in her eyes.

"What is it?" she asked, hurrying to her. "What's wrong?"

"It's Paul!"

"The boy you were telling me about?"

Val nodded.

"What's he done? Gotten himself busted?"

"It's worse than that. He's dead!"

"You've got to be kidding!"

"They've been telling about it on the news. There was a car accident, and he was killed!" Numbly she related what had happened, even telling about the girl who was killed with him.

Betty put her arms around Valerie and held her while she sobbed. She didn't tell her what she was thinking, that it was a good thing Val had broken up with him or she would be the dead girl in the car. There would be time enough for that later. Right now, she needed someone to comfort her, to help her bear her grief. It was some time before Val was able to get control of herself enough to talk.

"And they think I was with him because they–they found my ring on her finger."

"How did that happen?"

"I–I gave the ring to Paul," the girl went on. "He said it meant so much to him he was going to wear it always. He bought a silver chain and wore it around his neck. And he gave me this charm."

Betty looked at it without comment.

"He must have given my ring to that–that other girl," Val continued. "That's the only way she could have gotten it." She stared wildly at Betty. "And now they're both dead!"

The older girl voiced a concern that Val hadn't even thought about.

"I know you've been uptight about your parents, but do you realize what this is doing to them?"

She sat up and wiped her eyes. "What do you mean?"

"They think you're the one who was killed in the accident."

Valerie nodded. That was what the announcer had said, but at the time she hadn't fully understood what it meant.

"You don't want them to think that, do you?"

Val did not reply. Even though she knew her mom and dad didn't love her, she loved them and didn't want to see them hurt.

"What do you think I ought to do?"

Betty did not answer her immediately.

"What should I do?" the other girl repeated.

"You know what you have to do," she said quietly.

"No!" Val exclaimed. "I can't go home and face them!"

CHAPTER 10

"I'M FREE NOW"

Betty made some coffee for Val, and they sat at the table for an hour talking. From time to time, the tears came as the younger girl thought about Paul's death.

"I did like him," she sobbed. "I liked him a lot."

"I'm sure you did."

"He wasn't what everyone said he was. He was really a beautiful person."

"I know exactly what you mean," Betty answered, making no attempt to stop her crying. "He sounds exactly like a friend I had once."

"He does?" Val looked up, surprised and somehow drawn to Betty because of a common bond. "Where is he now?"

She raised her head, her eyes staring at some distant horizon. "He's dead, too, Val."

"He–he is?" The question in her voice asked for more information.

She nodded. "An overdose. Somebody sold him pure heroin, and the stuff killed him."

"I–I'm sorry. Really I am."

Betty smiled. "Don't be. He's the reason I'm like this." She gestured helplessly. "He got me to popping H and then mainlining it. I loved the guy, but he put these chicken tracks on my arm."

After a time, the conversation turned to Val's parents and their reaction to the accident.

"Have you decided what you're going to do about them?" Betty asked.

Val eyed her blankly. She had been so concerned over Paul's death she hadn't even thought about her parents and Bill. Even now, she didn't see that she had any special obligation to them. She was the one who suffered the loss. Not them.

"What about my parents?"

"They think you're dead."

The younger girl gasped. She hadn't thought of that.

"That's right," Betty continued. "They've identified your ring, so they think you're the girl who was wearing it. According to the newscast, they've already accepted the fact that you're dead."

"They'll find out I'm not," Val said lamely.

"But when? After they've had a funeral for you? After they've grieved for you for a week or a month or two months? How long will it be before they learn the truth?"

The younger girl flinched. This was something she hadn't counted on. She was convinced that her parents didn't love her, but she didn't want to hurt them. Not that much, anyway.

"Won't the police keep hunting until they find out who the dead girl is?" she asked.

"They will if there's some reason for them to keep looking, but if they are as convinced as your parents seem to be that you were killed in the car accident, they will close the case and stop investigating. If they do that, your parents may go on for the rest of their lives thinking you're dead. You wouldn't want that, would you?"

Val shuddered. "But what can I do?"

Betty squinted narrowly at her. "You could call them and tell them you're all right."

"Oh, I couldn't do that."

"Why not?"

"It would only cause trouble." When she saw that her friend did not understand, she continued. "You don't know my parents. They'd start hounding me to tell them where I am so they could come get me." She replied heatedly. "I broke out of the neat little box they were forcing me into, and I'm not going back!" Frustration and helplessness broke the hard set to her mouth. "Don't you understand? I can't have them pressuring me again!"

Her friend poured another cup of coffee. "I know exactly what you're trying to say," she answered. "I had the same problems at home and left for the same reasons."

"Then you *know* I can't call them and have them force me to come home."

"I didn't say that." She got a match as though to light a cigarette but held it in her hand. "I'm older than you are, Val, and I've been away from home a lot longer than you have. It's been more than five years since I've seen my parents. But if I was in your place and they thought I was dead, I'd be on that phone right away." She paused, the lights dimming in her eyes. "I've already hurt them far too much. I wouldn't want to torture them the way you're torturing your mom and dad."

"But I can't call them!"

"Why not?" her older friend retorted coldly. "You know the number, don't you?"

"Yes."

"Then you'd better call them. You could have caused one or the other to have a heart attack already."

Val's eyes rounded. "Do you really think so?"

"You know the friend I was telling you about? The one who got an overdose? His mother had a coronary the night before his funeral and died two days later."

Reluctantly she picked up the phone and called her parents' home in Rock Point. She was so frightened she almost hung up when it started to ring, but Betty put out her hand and stopped her.

"Go ahead! You'll feel better if you call."

Bill was the one who answered. At first, he could scarcely believe it was her.

"Val!" he exclaimed. "Val!"

"Who is it, Bill?" his mother demanded, hurrying to the phone.

"Val! Is that you? Val!" He was so excited he could say nothing more for a moment or two. "Mom! Dad! It's Valerie!"

He sounded so relieved and so glad to talk to her that she began to cry. She could hear her mother crying, too, and trying to take the phone so she could talk to her. But Bill wouldn't let her have it.

"Where are you?" he asked insistently. "Are you in town?"

She did not answer his question.

"I–I saw the news about the car accident on television this morning. I heard that mom and dad think I was the girl in the car, but I wasn't. I thought I'd better call and tell you and mom and dad that I'm all right."

"Thank God!" he breathed.

"Where is she, Bill?" Irene wanted to know. "Is she all right?"

She reached for the phone again. This time Bill would have given it to her, but she swayed and almost fell. Her husband stepped forward to catch her. He held her for a moment or two, talking softly to her.

Bill continued to talk with Valerie. He finally persuaded her to tell him she was in Denver staying at the apartment of a friend. He could hear an ambulance siren and the roar of heavy trucks in the background.

"Come home, Val," Bill pleaded.

"I'm free now," she insisted, "and that's the way I'm going to stay, so you'd just as well forget it."

By this time Bart and Irene Anderson had regained their composure, and Bart wrenched the phone from his son's hand.

"Now, Valerie!" he roared, his voice taut and shaking with emotion. "We've been so worried about you, we've all been sick! Worried isn't the word! We've all thought you were dead! The whole town thinks you're dead!"

"I'm sorry, Dad!" Her voice was icy.

"If you hadn't called, we'd have held a funeral service for you."

"I know." Her voice trembled. "That's the reason I called. I didn't want you to worry about me."

"You didn't want us to worry? Now, don't give me that! If you hadn't wanted us to worry, you'd never have left home in the first place."

Only her silence answered him.

"I know things may not have been too good for you around here," he continued, "but–but we'll make it up to you. You won't have to worry about that. Things will be different when you come home. I guarantee it."

"But I can't come home, Daddy!" she blurted. "That isn't why I called. I only wanted to let you know that I'm alive and all right."

He was intent on finishing what he started to say. "I'll see to it that Bill doesn't talk to you about that stupid religion of his anymore. I know that's the reason you ran away. You couldn't stand that sort of thing. And I don't blame you. He about drives me nuts with it too. But you won't have to worry about it. I'll see it won't happen again."

She hadn't liked having her brother preach at her, that was true. But she couldn't have her dad thinking she'd run away because of Bill. It wasn't that at all.

"It wasn't Bill's fault, Daddy," she protested. She was about to tell him it was his and Mom's and–and Paul's for not wanting to have anything more to do with her, but she couldn't bring herself to say any more on the subject.

Her dad wasn't listening to her anyway. That was one of the reasons they didn't get along. He *never* heard what she was trying to tell him. At the moment he was trying to argue her into coming back home. When pleading and promises didn't work, he turned hard.

"Now listen to me, Val!" he snapped. "I've had about all of this from you I'm going to take. You've worried your mother and me so much the last week it's a wonder we both haven't been in the hospital. You've got to stop this nonsense right now and get back here! Do you understand?"

For ten or fifteen seconds all he could hear on the phone was her labored breathing. Then the line went dead. Slowly he turned to face his wife and son.

"She hung up!" he muttered. "She actually hung up on me!"

"What did you expect?" his wife snapped. "You hammered and hammered at her until she couldn't take it anymore, just like you always do. I don't blame her for hanging up on you!"

"That's the trouble around here. You always take her side in everything. I try to correct her and what happens? You ruffle your feathers like an old mother hen!"

Tears were standing in Irene's eyes, held back momentarily by her anger. "How could you correct her? You're never home! You live at that tavern."

"Look who's talkin'! You spend all your time playing bingo when you should be at home taking care of your family."

"Maybe it would be better if you played bingo once in a while. At least you wouldn't be coming home so smashed you don't even know what day it is!"

They continued to argue angrily. At last, however, Bart broke it off and reached for the phone.

"What are you going to do, Dad?" Bill asked.

"I'm going to call the cops. They've got to know Val's alive!"

"Do you think they'll keep looking for her?" his wife wanted to know.

"You can bet on that!" he called police headquarters. "If she won't listen to reason when I talk to her, maybe being picked up by the police and spending a couple of nights in jail will do it! I'm not having her defy everything I tell her!"

CHAPTER 11

BILL GOES TO DENVER

Bill knew his father had to let the authorities know Valerie was still alive, and he had to tell them she called the house from Denver. But he didn't like the idea of leaving the full responsibility for finding her to the police. He knew how he would feel if he were in her place and the family didn't do anything about getting him to come back. He'd think they really didn't want him.

He was afraid Val had that idea already. When he talked to her on the phone she sounded as though she thought everyone in the family had turned against her.

"Why don't we do something ourselves about getting her back here, Dad?" he asked.

Bart Anderson bristled defensively. "And exactly how do I go about doing that?"

"We could go to Denver and try to find her."

"That's a job for the cops. They know how to go about it."

"We could look for her too. I'm afraid if the police find her and force her to come back home, she'll just run away again the first chance she gets."

"If we do find her and she doesn't want to come home, what then? If you're not going to force her to come back, do we leave her there? She's just a kid, you know. Fourteen years old! What she needs is a few good strappings to let her know there are some things she's *got* to do! Let the cops find her and throw her in for a few hours. Let her find out what happens to kids who don't mind their fathers!"

"If we try to find her," Bill continued, "at least she'd know we love her and want her back."

"I can't take time off my job." Bart Anderson was so upset he was mad at everyone. "I've got to work to keep this house going. I can't run all over Denver trying to find a brat of a kid who doesn't care any more about us than Val does."

"Of course, she's only your daughter!" his wife exploded. "You can't compare her with your job or that wonderful paycheck you bring home."

"All right!" He whirled to face her. "How am I supposed to find Val? Answer me that!"

They started to argue once more, but Bill stopped them. "I could go and look for her, Dad," he suggested.

"You wouldn't be any better at it than I would," he said defensively.

"Maybe not, but I could try. And if I should find her, I think she might listen to me right now more than she would to you. She was mad at you just now."

His dad turned slowly, his great fists clenched. "I suppose you think you can do more with her than I can!"

Irene Anderson grasped the lapels of her husband's jacket. "Please, Bart! Please!"

He put his hands on her wrists to push her away, but the hurt in her eyes was so great he pulled her close instead. For a while, he held her in his arms, something Bill had never remembered seeing before. It seemed that much of the bitterness and anger of the past melted in those few brief seconds.

"Do you *really* think we ought to let Bill go and look for her?" Bart asked brokenly.

She nodded. "I would like to have him try."

They went over to the couch and sat down, discussing the matter in detail. Once Bart had pushed his pride aside, he agreed with his wife and son that it would be better for Bill to look for Val, along with the police. Mrs. Anderson thought she should go along, but they talked her out of it.

"If Val should call home again," Bart told her, "or even come home, there should be someone here to talk to her."

She could see the wisdom of that. "But I do think you ought to go right away, Bill. I can't rest until she's safe at home again."

"I'll go right away."

Bill's parents insisted he get someone to go with him. He didn't like the idea of taking the time to locate a guy who could go along, but it would be better, he realized. At least he would have someone to talk things over with.

The first ones he thought of were Doug and Del Davis. It was Saturday, and he didn't know what they would be doing. Sometimes Del helped Danny at the airport on weekends. Bill drove out to the airport and talked with Del. Getting permission to take the day off was no problem. In half an hour they were on their way, tooling down the freeway toward Denver.

"Where do you think we ought to start looking?" Del asked as they pulled into the city.

Bill had been thinking about that ever since they left Rock Point. It would be difficult enough finding a missing person in his hometown. Denver could be almost impossible.

"We've got a few leads," he replied. "When I talked with her on the phone, I heard an ambulance siren and some heavy trucks going by. She was calling from along a busy through street."

"Unfortunately, there are two or three of those in Denver," Del replied.

Bill laughed. "Of course, we know she doesn't have much money, so she won't be in places where it costs a lot. That cuts down the area quite a bit."

"Who does she know in Denver?"

"That's one of the things that's got us beat. We only know of two of her friends who live in Denver now. Mom called both of them, but they hadn't seen or heard anything from her."

"But she said she was staying in the apartment of a friend, didn't she?"

"That's what she said, but lately we haven't been able to believe anything she tells us."

They were sitting at a stoplight waiting for green when he thought of Paul Keller. Paul was dead, that was true, but Bill decided Val might have gone into the area where the same type of kids lived. There was a place like that in Denver. Every city had one.

"I've got an idea, Del." He made a left turn and headed for the rundown district where the bohemians and drug users hung out. As he drove, both he and Del were praying silently. Denver was huge. How could they realistically expect to find her?

Bill and Del drove up and down the streets that bordered the poorer section of the downtown Denver business district. They stopped a number of kids in dirty jeans and sweatshirts and asked about her, showing them her picture. Once or twice, Bill thought he saw recognition showing in the eyes of the kids he talked with, as though they actually had seen her, but they protested strongly that they hadn't.

"No," one guy said. "I know most of the kids on the street, but I haven't seen this one around." His eyes sized up Bill. "Why do you want her? What's she to you?"

"She's my sister."

Del was sure the other boy knew much more about Valerie than he claimed. Del mentioned his suspicion to Bill when they were alone again.

"I had the same idea. Maybe he does know something we don't."

"I'm convinced of it."

"But how are we going to get him to tell us? That's what I'd like to know."

"We could go to the police. Maybe they could haul in some of these kids and scare them into telling us what they know."

Bill thought about that. He knew how the kids on the street hung together. "I'm afraid they'd keep saying they didn't know anything until the police gave up questioning them. They'd know the police couldn't hold them very long. And, if Val got word that the police were asking about her, she might get scared and run again."

"You might be right, at that." For the first time Del's discouragement showed through.

They spent the rest of the day alternately driving around and walking the streets looking for Valerie. They talked to endless numbers of teenagers without getting any solid information about her.

Everyone claimed not to know anything about her. Finally, tired and discouraged, they went to a motel for the night. Early the next morning they began their search again.

"What are we going to do today?" Del asked.

"I don't know how much longer we ought to keep looking for her on our own. What do you say we spend the morning the same as we did yesterday. If we don't find her by noon, we can go to the police and see if they will help us."

"I thought you wanted to find her yourself, Bill."

"I do, but we aren't getting anywhere, that's for sure."

They went back to the small area where they had concentrated their search the afternoon before and continued to look for her and ask questions. About midmorning a gaunt-featured girl in her early twenties approached them.

"Hello."

They both turned and waited.

"Are you the ones looking for the kid from Rock Point? The one whose parents thought she was killed in that car accident the other night?"

"Do you know her?" Bill asked. "Can you tell us where she is?"

"Maybe." Her smile was inscrutable.

"We've spent half of yesterday and the whole morning trying to find her. We're about to give up and go to the police."

"Leave the cops out of this. Now listen, what's Val to you?"

"She's my sister!" Bill retorted. He felt like grabbing her by the shoulders and shaking the answers from her. "Where is she? Is she all right?"

"Yeah, yeah, she's okay." Betty's smile showed amusement. "But I don't know how long she will be."

"Exactly what do you mean by that?" Bill asked.

"Calm down. You want the picture? Here it is. The jerks who hang around my place have all got their eyes on her. I don't know how long it's going to be until somebody talks her into trying weed or acid." She paused.

'When I heard that someone was looking for her, I had a hunch it was her family. I'm headed for my place right now. You can come along if you want to."

Bill and Del looked at each other. They didn't find it easy to trust this girl with her tough manner. Betty saw their hesitation.

She spun angrily. "Listen to me! I could have left your sister on the street where I found her. No skin off my nose if she messes up her life good. I don't like it when you sticklers get so uptight all of a sudden. If you want to see your sister, let's go. If not, I've got better things to do than watching you blow your cool." She started up the street abruptly. The boys followed her, stunned into silence by Betty's fury.

"Do you think Val will talk to me?" Bill asked as they crossed the street.

Betty shrugged. "Who knows? Maybe she will.

Or maybe she'll say it's a bad scene and leave you standin' in the hall."

The boys were not prepared for the dingy stairwell that led to Betty's apartment, the worn, creaking steps, and the dirty walls covered with crude messages. An unpleasant smell filled the hallway. Bill shuddered. It horrified him to think of Val living in such a depressing place.

Betty must have known what he was thinking.

She inserted her key in the lock and was about to open the door when she stopped and turned to face him.

"You wait here. I'll go in and have Val come out to talk to you."

"Wouldn't it be better to talk with her inside?" Bill asked. The filthy hall made him uneasy.

"If it was better to go in," Betty snarled, "I'd tell you. I want to get this kid out of here as much as you do. All you've got to do is wait here. Val will come out and talk to you."

"But–" he protested.

Anger burned in her dark eyes. "We do this my way, got it?"

By this time Bill was as furious as she was. Days of worry and frustration had worn away his characteristic patience. Del saw Bill's anger and took hold of his arms as a silent restraint. He was not sure his friend read the depth of Betty's hostility or the trouble it could cause them. It was better to be cautious. It might even be safer for them in the hall.

When Betty saw that Bill and Del had accepted her edict and would stay outside, she opened the door and slipped inside the apartment. The door was open for only an instant, but they glimpsed a narrow wedge of the living room.

It was as dark and as barren as the hallway, except for a few pieces of battered furniture. Kids were sitting on the bare wooden floor. The air was a cloud of sweet, acrid smoke.

Del thought Bill was going to charge through the door in spite of what Betty had said, but at that instant his sister appeared.

"What're you doing here?" she demanded, staring at her brother and Del.

CHAPTER 12

BETTY'S VICTORY

Bill and his sister faced each other. Their eyes met and then turned away, retreating in embarrassment. A moment before, Bill had known what he would say to her. It had been all worked out in his mind in the past day and a half. He had planned to flash a warm appealing smile when he urged her to come home with him and Del. Now, however, the words scattered, overwhelmed by his emotion of relief. He could say nothing.

Valerie pulled the door shut behind her, muffling the wild beat of the music. It felt strange to see Bill here, and she began to see the dirt and dinginess again, as if from his eyes. She felt a gladness at the sight of Bill, almost wanting to cry.

"Well," she began, nervously, "What do you want of me?"

He cleared his throat.

"We've been worried about you, Val."

She glanced down at the floor, saying nothing.

"It's the truth. Mom and Dad are about sick with worry."

"I can see that. They're worried so much about me that you had to come and look for me. They're so worried Dad's probably getting smashed and Mom's off somewhere playing bingo."

"That's where you're wrong." Bill was praying inwardly for wisdom in talking with her. He knew he needed restraint, too, so he wouldn't lose his temper and make matters worse.

"Both Mom and Dad have been so concerned about you I've been worried about them. Particularly Mom. She's been having a rough time. I don't think she's been to one bingo game since you left."

Val waited uncomfortably. "The police came and told us about the accident. We saw your ring and thought you'd been killed. That really hit Mom hard."

"You make it sound as though it was my fault," Val broke in. "I didn't have anything to do with that accident, and I certainly didn't tell the police to go to mom and dad. So you can't blame me."

"Of course, no one would even have thought you were killed in the accident if you'd been home when it happened," he reminded her.

"Well, I called you the next day, didn't I?" Val was beginning to feel defensive. "Look, did you come here just to tell me I'm a creep?"

Bill paused a moment. Then he continued more gently.

"I know things haven't been easy for you around home."

"Then you can understand why I cut out."

"Yes," said Bill slowly. "I think I can. I've had my times, too, when I've wanted to leave. I guess for a long time it was football that kept me from going."

Val looked at Bill and felt an instant of new closeness to him.

"But look," he said, changing his tone of voice. "Del and I are here to see if you'll come home with us."

"Why should I? Nobody cares anything about me." But Val's resistance was lowering.

"That's not true. Mom and Dad want you to come home. I want you. Please don't turn us down, Val." He was pleading with her.

She hesitated. There were times when she thought she could not stand another hour in Betty's apartment. Right now, she was sick of the parade of kids who hung around the place and was disgusted with the things they did. She didn't think she could stand it with them any longer. She wasn't sure she wanted to go home, however.

"And what if I don't want to go home?" she demanded.

Bill avoided answering her directly. "We all want you to come."

She moved a step or two away from the door,

thoughtfully. "I can't go back to Rock Point after what happened," she murmured. "I–I'd be pointed at by the whole town."

"That's not true, Val," Del Davis broke in. "Nobody's going to point at you. The people I know want to help you if they can."

"I'll bet they do! They want to get me spaced out on religion the way you and Bill are!"

"God can solve your problems, Val," her brother told her. "He solves mine."

Anger flashed in her eyes. "So what has God done for our family? And for me? The only guy I've ever had care about me drops me for another girl and then he gets killed in a car wreck. And now everybody knows about it."

"Nobody thinks anything about what's happened to you, Val," Bill assured her. When he saw the doubt in her features he turned to his companion. "Do they, Del?"

"Of course not. I haven't heard anyone say anything about it except to be concerned for you."

"They'll say plenty to me," she countered.

Bill hesitated, wondering if this was the moment to explain about God's love for her in spite of all the problems and tragedy Val was experiencing. Her next statement stunned him.

"You can tell mom and dad I'm getting along fine," she informed him curtly, "but you'll have to make it clear to them that I'm not going to come home.

I've thought it all out and made up my mind. I'll get a job and earn my own way. They can forget I was ever in the family."

As Bill and Val were talking, Betty had opened the door and come out in the hall. When the younger girl finally stopped talking, Betty spoke up.

"Listen Val, your time's up here."

The younger girl turned to face Betty, bewildered by the sudden change in her friend.

"But–"

"You've got three minutes to get in there, get your junk packed, and ship out!"

Still Valerie stared at her. She couldn't understand what had happened. "But I've decided to stay here with you."

"Your time's up!" repeated Betty firmly. "You're moving out."

"But I'm going to get a job, Betty. I'll pay my own way!"

"Not here," the older girl replied. "Get in there and get your stuff."

Val still had not moved.

"If you know what's good for you, you'll go back home with your brother and stay there, at least until you get out of high school. Listen, babes, you don't want to end up like me!"

Betty hadn't intended to say that. The words had slipped out. As they did, tears ran down her cheeks.

"Val, you're a nice kid, and I like you. But I can't

let you stay around here and throw your life away like I have."

She turned her head to keep the others from seeing her tears.

"But you're really cool, and I'd like to be just like you!" Val exclaimed loyally.

"You don't know what you're saying, girl." Betty took Val by the hand and started back into the apartment. "Come on, I'll help you pack."

Val was crying, too, as she went inside with her friend. Del and Bill stared at each other in the semi-darkness of the hall, stunned by what had happened. They hadn't expected Betty to succeed where they failed.

A moment or two later the two girls were back with Valerie's suitcase. Betty put her arms around the younger girl and kissed her impulsively.

"Listen, kid, you're so lucky to have a brother like Bill who cares enough to come looking for you. He had a mean time out there on the street. I don't know anything about that religion of his you were talking about, but if it makes him like he is, it might be worth a try."

She let Val go at last, wiping at her eyes.

"And don't you *ever* run away again, or I'll come and clobber you. See?"

The two boys and Val went down the rickety stairs and walked in the direction of the parked car. She was silent until they reached the first street corner.

"Don't you ever say one word against Betty!" she warned them. "Not one word!"

"You don't have to worry about that," Bill told her.

He stopped and called their parents to tell them he had found Val and they were on their way home. None of the three spoke as they reached the car, got in, and drove toward the freeway.

Val slouched down in the seat, her gaze fixed on the distant stop light. What Betty had said about Bill touched her deeply. Now that she thought about it, she realized that Bill did care about her. *He didn't have to come here and look for me,* Val thought. *He never used to care about me. Maybe his religion has made a difference.* Val had talked with Bill enough to know he gave Jesus Christ the credit for making any change that had come into his life in recent days.

He had talked about the way he used to live and called it sin. The Bible said, Bill had explained, that it earned him death, the same as anyone else who was without Christ.

"'Yes, all have sinned; all fall short of God's glorious ideal,'" Bill had read to her, "'Yet now God declares us "not guilty" of offending him if we trust in Jesus Christ, who in his kindness freely takes away our sins. For God sent Christ Jesus to take the punishment for our sins and to end all God's anger against us.'"[1*]

Val didn't understand much of what it meant to be a Christian, but there was the beginning of a longing within her. Someday, maybe–

---

1   *Romans 3:23, 25 The Living Bible.

THE DANNY ORLIS SERIES

The Danny Orlis series, by Bernard Palmer, delivers a blend of adventure, mystery, and suspense through various settings—from the Canadian wilderness to Guatemalan jungles. Danny Orlis, an adept outdoorsman, skilled athlete, and committed Christian, employs his quick thinking, calm bravery, and biblical solutions to confront everyday problems and hair-raising dangers. Early stories focus on Danny navigating school life, sports, and outdoor challenges, while in later books, Danny and his wife Kay provide wisdom and guidance to youngsters facing lifelike situations and challenges. Having sold over two million copies, this series has made Palmer a renowned author in Christian youth literature. Palmer is also the author of the Felicia Cartright series and various other series for Christian youth.

AVAILABLE FROM WWW.ANEKOPRESS.COM